The Wrong Words

Written by Liz Minister
Illustrated by Paula Martyr

Chapter 1

Daryl woke up very early on his birthday. He couldn't wait to see what Uncle Max had sent him.

Uncle Max always gave him amazing presents. One year he had given him a special pair of glasses so he could see in the dark. Last year Uncle Max had given him roller skates with motors in each wheel.

Daryl hurried downstairs. In the hall, he found a big brown box with an envelope on it addressed to him. He read the birthday card inside.

Happy Birthday Daryl!
Please look after Merry the robot. She can walk but I haven't had time to teach her to talk. She likes jokes and rhymes, so have fun teaching her. I hope you have a very happy birthday.
Love,
Uncle Max x
P.S. Can you say this tongue-twister? Three thieves threw trumpets through trees.

Daryl tore open the big box. He
soon found the robot and removed
her carefully from the box. He
couldn't wait to tell her some of
his jokes.

Daryl played with Merry every day, but even after three weeks she still couldn't speak. Daryl had read lots of rhymes to Merry and told her lots of jokes.

'What's the difference between a robber and a church bell?' he asked her one morning. Merry didn't answer.

'It's easy,' said Daryl, answering his own joke. 'One steals from the people and the other peals from the steeple!'

But Merry didn't even smile.

Daryl's mum said it had taken Daryl years to learn to talk. Now she wished she'd never taught him because he never shut up!

Once, after Daryl had told Merry a very funny joke, he thought he'd heard a giggle. Maybe it had just been his old bed creaking.

Then one morning, when Daryl woke up, Merry was sitting on his bed! She was speaking in a slow robot voice and he was surprised!

She said, 'Knock – knock.'

Daryl sat up, smiling. 'Who's there?' he asked Merry.

'Daryl,' she replied.

'Daryl who?' he asked.

'Daryl – be – your – robot – talking!' said Merry.

'Oh yes!' said Daryl, punching the
air like footballers on the television.
'Daryl be…that will be your robot
talking! You can talk!'

Daryl tried a joke on Merry.
'Knock, knock,' he said.

Merry replied, 'Who's – there?'

'Irish stew,' said Daryl.

'Irish – stew – who?'
asked Merry.

'Irish stew in the name of the
law!' said Daryl.

Merry's laughter was a
funny sound.

Clunk – click – clunk, went Merry's dials. 'Why – did – the – robber – get – caught – stealing – a – big – clock?' she asked.

Daryl knew the answer to that one. 'He took too much time!' he answered.

'What – do – you – call – a – boy – who – steals – hamburgers?' asked Merry. Daryl didn't know.

'A – hamburglar!' replied Merry, and both she and Daryl burst out laughing.

Daryl's mum came into his room.

'Merry can talk and she knows some brilliant jokes,' said Daryl. 'Wait till you hear this.'

Daryl asked Merry, 'Do robots have brothers?'

Quick as a flash, Merry replied, 'No - only - transistors!'

'Oh no!' said Mum, 'not two of you telling me corny jokes. I don't think I can stand it!'

Then Merry looked at Daryl and said, 'Carol?'

'My name's Daryl, he said, laughing. 'Carol is a girl's name.'

'Daryl – Carol – barrel,' said Merry, 'all – the – same.'

'What do you mean?' asked Daryl, puzzled. Then he realised why Merry didn't understand. 'They sound the same, but they don't mean the same thing. You've got a lot to learn,' he told Merry.

Daryl and Merry became best friends.

Sometimes, when Merry got excited or nervous, her words came out in the wrong order. Daryl would work out what she was trying to say.

One day, Merry said, 'I – very – am – hungry. What – is – today – tea – for?'

'I think you mean: *I am very hungry. What is for tea today?*' said Daryl. 'What would you like?'

'Not poodles,' said Merry.

'Good,' said Daryl. 'We don't eat dogs!' Then Daryl realised that Merry had meant to say *pot noodles*. 'You are a robot funny!' joked Daryl.

'You – thank,' said Merry, shyly.

Chapter 2

One day, Merry was alone in the house when there was a knock at the door.

Merry called out, 'Knock – knock' and she opened the door. There were two men.

'Get out of our way, you stupid robot,' growled one of them, pushing her aside.

Merry had no idea what the men wanted. She couldn't understand why they were being nasty to her.

'Quick, mate,' said the other man, 'now's a good chance to rob the place.'

'What – kind – of – robbery – is – the – least – dangerous?' stuttered Merry.

'What is that daft robot saying now?' asked one of the robbers.

'It's just talking rubbish,' said the other.

'A – safe – robbery,' muttered Merry. Neither of the robbers was listening. They were busy stuffing jewellery and other things into a bag.

'What – did – the – policeman –
say – to – his – tummy?' said
Merry, quietly.

'Can't we turn that thing off?'
said one of the robbers.

'YOU'RE – UNDER – A -
VEST!' said Merry, in her loudest
voice. 'YOU'RE – UNDER – A
VEST!' she kept repeating.

The robbers looked up. They
didn't like the sound of that at all.
And they didn't like the odd look
on the robot's face.

'Let's get out of here,' said one of the robbers.

'That robot gives me the creeps,' said the other.

So the two robbers dashed out of the front door, carrying a bag which had all Mum's jewellery in it and more! They left the house in a mess and did not shut the front door.

Merry sat down on the stairs feeling very miserable. She hadn't known how to stop the robbers. 'Me – robot – useless,' she said, sadly.

When Daryl came home from school, he was surprised to find the door open. He thought maybe Merry had gone for a walk, but he hoped not. Merry still didn't know her way round, so he was glad to find her sitting on the stairs.

'Hey, Merry,' said Daryl, 'I've just heard a brilliant new joke. Why are robots never afraid?' Daryl was surprised when Merry said nothing, so he gave her the answer, 'Because they have nerves of steel!'

Merry still said nothing. Daryl thought she looked strange. Then he noticed the lights on her control panel looked very dim.

'What's up?' asked Daryl. 'Here's another joke. This will make you laugh. What do police fish ride in?' When Merry didn't reply, Daryl went on, 'A squid car!' But Merry didn't even smile.

Daryl went upstairs to get his joke book. He noticed that his mum's dressing table drawers were open. One drawer was empty. All the jewellery had gone. The room looked a mess. 'Oh no! What's happened?' thought Daryl.

He ran downstairs to ask Merry what had happened, and where the jewellery had gone.

'Have you taken Mum's jewellery?' he asked her.

'Knock! Knock!' said Merry.

'Not now,' said Daryl, crossly. 'This is serious. What's happened to Mum's room and her jewellery?'

Before Merry could say anything, Mum arrived home. Daryl showed her the mess and the empty drawer. She was very upset.

'I think Merry knows something about it,' said Daryl, and he went back downstairs to talk to Merry. 'Have you taken Mum's jewellery?' asked Daryl.

'Under – a – vest,' said Merry.

'Under a vest?' asked Daryl. 'What does that mean? Is that where you've hidden it?' But Merry wouldn't say anything more.

'It's no good,' said Daryl, when he went back upstairs to Mum. 'I think Merry may have hidden your jewellery. She wouldn't have stolen it. But she's muddled her words so I can't work out where it might be.'

'Well, we can't keep a robot who takes things, even if it is just to hide them.' Mum sounded cross and she stormed out of the room.

Chapter 3

Merry kept saying silly things.
'Knock – knock!' said Merry.

'Who's there?' said Daryl.

'Two – mad – ben!' said Merry.

'Two mad ben who?' said Daryl.

'Knock – knock! Two – mad – ben!' repeated Merry, over and over again.

Daryl went to tell his mum what Merry had been saying. 'Her wiring must be wrong,' suggested Daryl. 'Let's call Uncle Max.'

When Uncle Max arrived, he was very puzzled. He spoke to Merry sternly.

'Now, Merry, I want a straight answer. Where are all the things?'

'Knock – knock,' said Merry. 'Two – mad – ben. Roll – the – stings. Under – a – vest. Talk – rubbish.'

'Well, you're right about the last bit,' said Uncle Max, crossly. 'You're certainly talking rubbish.' He was very annoyed.

'I'm sorry,' he said to Mum and Daryl. 'I'll have to take Merry away. I think she may have taken the jewellery somewhere, but I can't get any sense out of her.'

Daryl watched Uncle Max packing Merry away in her box. 'Knock, knock,' said Daryl, hoping to cheer her up with a joke. But Merry didn't reply.

That night, Daryl went to bed feeling sad. He missed Merry's jokes and he even missed the funny way she muddled her words. He couldn't believe that she might be a thief. She just couldn't be! 'Let's hope Uncle Max can sort her out,' thought Daryl.

He lay in bed staring at the glow-in-the-dark stars, but he couldn't sleep. He was tossing and turning. He kept thinking about the things Merry had said since the burglary.

Daryl repeated the words to himself, hoping they were just another puzzle to solve: *Knock, knock.* Was she telling him a joke? he thought. Why else might she say, *knock, knock*?

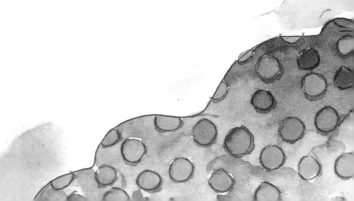

Suddenly, Daryl sat up in bed. 'Of course,' he said aloud. 'I bet she heard someone knocking at the door.'

Daryl's thoughts were racing, trying to remember what Merry had said next. Was it *two mad ben*? Perhaps she was trying to say *two bad men*.

Daryl felt he was getting somewhere: two bad men knocking at the door and…what had Merry said next? *Roll the stings*. Maybe she meant to say *stole the rings*!

Daryl jumped out of bed and ran downstairs to tell Mum.

'Mum! Mum! I think I've worked out what Merry was trying to say.' He told Mum about the bad men.

'I think you might be right, Daryl. But what did she mean by *under a vest*?'

'Mmm,' said Daryl, 'I haven't worked that bit out yet.'

'Quick, we'd better hurry,' said Mum. 'We'll have to stop Uncle Max before he takes Merry apart.'

Daryl and his mum jumped into the car. Daryl was still in his pyjamas. They had no time to lose.

Uncle Max was surprised to see them both on his doorstep and even more surprised to hear what they had to say.

'You're just in time,' he said. 'I was about to take Merry to bits.'

Uncle Max called the police station. Minutes later, a policeman called at the door. Uncle Max invited him in.

The policeman was very interested to hear about Merry's muddles.

'Well,' he said, 'this afternoon we arrested two men carrying a bag of stolen jewellery. When I said to them, "You're under arrest", one man turned to the other and said, "That daft robot must have told on us".'

'Clever old Merry,' said Daryl, 'Under a vest – under arrest.'

The next day, the policeman called at Daryl's home to return all of Mum's jewellery.

'I'm really proud of you,' Daryl told Merry.

'So am I,' said Mum, 'and I'm sorry I got cross with you.'

The lights on Merry's control panel twinkled brightly and she said, 'What – do – you – call – two – thieves?'

Mum and Daryl answered, 'I don't know. What do you call two thieves?'

'A – pair – of – nickers!' said Merry, laughing.

Daryl and Mum giggled, and even the policeman had to smile.